More Stories From

Panchatantra

SHREE

More Stories From PANCHATANTRA

ISBN 978-81-7963-025-9

© Publishers

Published by:
SHREE BOOK CENTRE

8 Kakad Industrial Estate - S. Keer Road (Off.L.J. Road)
Matunga West - MUMBAI 400 016 (India)
Tel : 24377516/24374559 Telefax : 91-22-24309183
E-mail : sales@shreebookcentre.com

Printed in India

CONTENTS

TITLE	PAGE NO.
1. The Lion And The Talking Den	5
2. The Jackal And The War Drum	13
3. The Owl And The Swan	19
4. The Snake And The Foolish Frogs	27
5. The Fox And The Grapes	33
6. The Brahmin And His Foolish Sons	41
7. The Tree That Talked	49
8. The Brahmin And His Dream	57
9. The Cap Seller And The Monkeys	65
10. The Crow And The Jackal	73
11. The Barber And The Saints	81
12. The Crane And The Crab	87

THE LION AND THE TALKING DEN

Once upon a time a clever jackal made his home in a cave in the jungle. Everyday he would leave the cave at sunrise in search of food and return at sunset.

In the same forest lived a lion. He had grown very old and could no longer run fast to catch his prey. He often went hungry because of this.

One day the lion tried to catch a lame deer. But even the lame deer could run faster than him.

As the lion wandered in search of prey, he saw the jackal's cave. He was sure that some animal lived in the cave. He had an idea!

The lion waited in the cave for the whole day. He was very hungry and this made him very restless and impatient.

At sunset the jackal came back to find the whole forest quiet around the cave. He was sure that some great danger lurked inside the cave. He thought of a plan and called out to the cave...

Hearing the clever jackal, the lion believed that the cave spoke to the jackal and called out in a hollow voice asking the jackal to come in. Hearing the roar of the lion, the jackal turned and ran for his life...

The lion waited for the jackal to enter. But soon realised that he had been fooled. He left the cave feeling very disappointed. The jackal watching from a safe distance, waited till the lion was out of sight and then returned to the cave for a good night's rest.

Moral: Haste is the bottom of all mistakes.

THE JACKAL AND THE WAR DRUM

Go away ! We don't want you with us anymore.

Once upon a time there lived a jackal. He was the leader of the pack. But none of the other jackals liked him. So one day they decided to chase him away.

The poor jackal wandered through the jungle. He felt very lonely. He was also hungry for he had not eaten for many days.

As he wandered through the jungle he suddenly heard a terrible noise. It was coming from behind a tree. The jackal ran for his life.

But after running some distance, the jackal realised that the noise had stopped. Then it came again and then it stopped.

The jackal was surprised and relieved to see that it was only an old war drum under the tree. Just then a branch of the tree moved in the breeze and brushed against the war drum. The terrible noise came again.

The jackal was delighted to find that there was a lot of food lying there. Some soldiers who had camped there had left both the war drum and the food behind.

Moral: Fortune favours the brave.

THE OWL AND THE SWAN

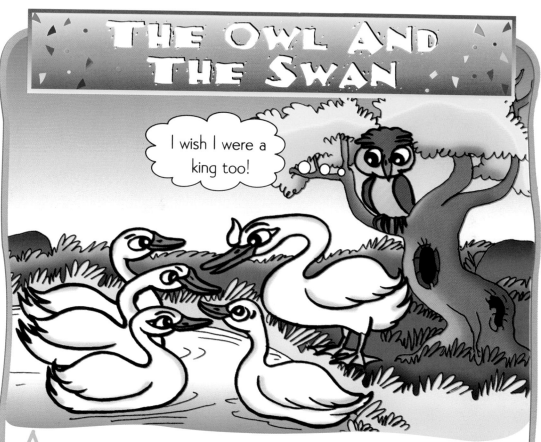

A swan and an owl once lived in the jungle. They were good friends. The swan was the king of swans, but the owl was just a common bird.

One day the owl woke up to see an army camp beneath his tree. Suddenly he had an idea! He quickly went to the swan and invited him to his tree.

Just then the captain gave the orders to the army to move. Hearing this the owl decided to show the swan his authority. He flew around the captain hooting loudly.

Now the captain was a man who believed in omens. He quickly decided that it was not a good day to travel.

The next morning the owl again invited the swan to show-off his kingdom. As the soldiers were getting ready to go, the owl flew around the captain's head hooting loudly.

But this time the captain was angry with the owl. He decided that he would set aside his fear of ill omens and continue with the journey. He called an archer.

The owl and the swan were perched on the same branch when the archer shot his arrow. The owl seeing the arrow, moved away hastily. But the swan was too slow to move...

The owl was filled with sadness and remorse at the loss of the noble swan. If he had not been so untruthful and vain glorious, he would not have caused the death of a good and honest friend.

Moral: Disaster follows pride.

THE SNAKE AND THE FOOLISH FROGS

There was a snake who was weak with old age. He could no longer hunt frogs and rats for his food as he used to.

Just then he saw a group of young frogs playing near a pond. They were lead by the prince of frogs. The old snake suddenly had an idea. When the curious frogs came closer he spoke to them gently.

The prince of frogs took the snake to his parents. The king and queen frogs decided to make the old snake their royal mount. The cunning snake allowed the king, queen and prince of frogs to ride on his back.

But soon the royal frogs realised that the snake moved too slowly. They called the snake and asked him why he could not move swiftly like the other snakes.

The next day the frog king summoned all the frogs together and made a proclamation that each day two frogs should go to the snake as his food.

In just a few days the snake had eaten many frogs in the pond. He was now strong and swift again. Then one day only the three royal frogs remained. He turned on them with a wicked hiss.

Moral: Do good to the villain, and he'll do evil to you.

THE FOX AND THE GRAPES

Oh! I wish I had some food. I have not eaten for many days.

Once in a jungle, there lived a fox. The fox was very hungry for he had not eaten for many days. He felt very weak and longed to find something to eat.

As the fox wandered around searching for food, he came to a village at the edge of the forest. There he saw a vineyard. There were big clusters of ripe grapes hanging from the vines.

The fox looked around to see if any one from the village was around. There was no one in sight. He squeezed himself into the vineyard through a hole in the hedge.

Not having eaten for many days, the poor fox feasted his eyes on the ripe, delicious looking grapes. But he soon realised that it was not within easy reach.

The fox jumped up with his mouth wide open to snap up a big bunch of grapes, but they were just beyond reach and his mouth closed over thin air.

But the hungry fox did not give up.
The sight of the ripe, juicy grapes was
too much for him. He moved back a
few paces so that he could run and
jump higher.

But the fox just could not jump high enough to reach the grapes. He was hungry and tired. Angry now, he caught hold of the poles holding up the vines and tried to shake them.

When even the shaking did not work, the fox at last gave up and turned to leave. As he was going he took a last look at grapes hanging on the vines. To cover his disappointment, the poor fox cursed the grapes.

Moral: What you don't get need not be bad.

Once upon a time, there lived an old and wise Brahmin. But the Brahmin's three sons were very foolish. They were very disunited and spent their days quarrelling. The old Brahmin was very worried for them.

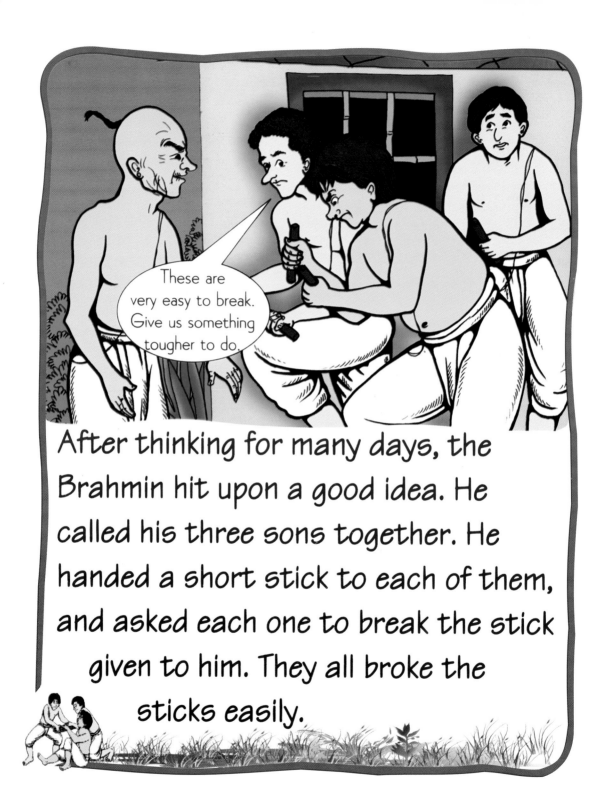

After thinking for many days, the
Brahmin hit upon a good idea. He
called his three sons together. He
handed a short stick to each of them,
and asked each one to break the stick
given to him. They all broke the
sticks easily.

The wise old Brahmin had known that his young sons would find it easy to break the single sticks. Now, as they watched curiously, he took three similar sticks and tied them together.

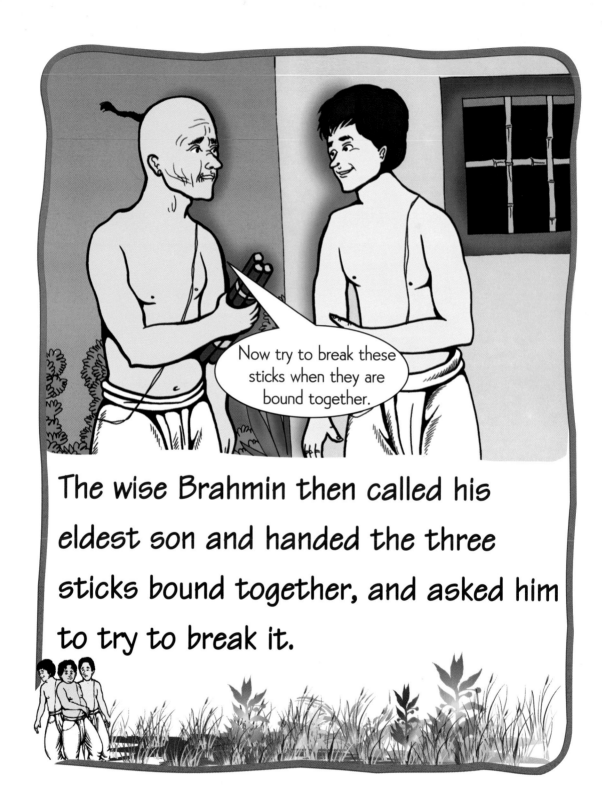

The wise Brahmin then called his eldest son and handed the three sticks bound together, and asked him to try to break it.

When the eldest son could not break the three sticks bound together, the old Brahmin called his second son and asked him to try to break the bundle of sticks.

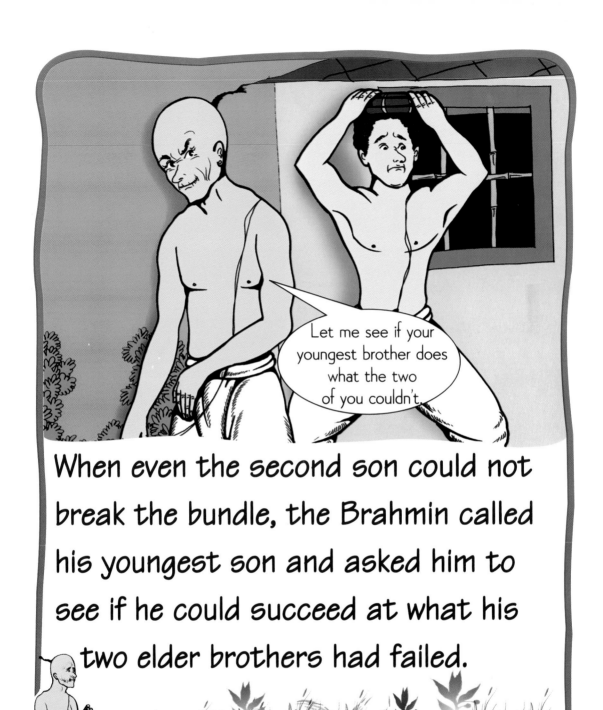

When even the second son could not break the bundle, the Brahmin called his youngest son and asked him to see if he could succeed at what his two elder brothers had failed.

When none of them could break the bundle, the old Brahmin asked them to join together and try to break the three sticks bound together.

When the brothers saw that they could not break the sticks which were tied into one bundle, they realised what their father was trying to teach them; that only if they could be united would they be strong enough to face life's difficulties.

Moral: United you stand, divided you fall.

THE TREE THAT TALKED

This is a good place for us to rest tonight.

Once, two friends, Pappabuddi and Dharmabuddi were travelling through a forest. They were going back home after selling their goods in a nearby town. They had all their money in one bag.

As darkness was falling, they decided to rest. It so happened that Pappabuddi was a very dishonest person and decided to cheat his friend of all the money. So he sat up hatching a plan while Dharmabuddi rested.

Pappabuddi thought of a plan. The next day he told Dharmabuddi that it might not be safe to travel with so much money. They could bury the money under a tree for safe keeping. Dharmabuddi agreed.

Soon the two friends were back home in their village. But that night, Pappabuddi came back alone and dug out the bag and took all the money for himself.

The following day, the two friends went back to dig out the money, and found that it had been stolen. Pappabuddi immediately accused his poor friend of the theft.

They went to the village elders. Pappabuddi insisted that Dharmabuddi had stolen the money. He even said that he had the tree spirit as witness. Hearing this, Dharmabuddi realised that it was all his friend's wicked plot.

So they all went to ask the tree spirit. It was all part of the Pappabuddi's plan. He had asked his old father to hide in the hollow trunk of the tree. Sure enough they all heard a voice in the tree saying that Dharmabuddi had stolen the money. The elders believed the voice.

But as they were talking, Dharmabuddi, who was not only honest but also very clever, picked some dry leaves and lit a fire under the tree trunk. In a short while, the old father jumped out coughing because of the smoke and accepted his son's guilt.

Moral: The greedy never prosper.

THE BRAHMIN AND HIS DREAM

Please accept this and bless my home O holy one!

There once lived a poor Brahmin. He was a priest in a small temple, and lived on the alms given by the people of the town he lived in. One day, a pious lady gave him a generous measure of wheat flour.

The poor Brahmin was very happy. He
went home and poured the
flour into an earthen pot and placed
it at the foot of his cot. He then lay
down and began to day dream.

The poor Brahmin dreamed that with the money he got from selling the flour, he would buy a goat.

He dreamt that he had made so much money with his goats that he bought a cow.

The poor Brahmin dreamed on that he had become so rich selling the cow's milk, that he bought himself a big house.

The Brahmin's dream seemed so real to him. He now dreamed that he got married to the beautiful daughter of a rich merchant.

In the Brahmin's dream a son was
born to him. He was proud that
he was the father of a beautiful son.

But his wife was not taking good care of their son. He was so angry, he kicked her. The Brahmin kicked out with his leg as he dreamed. He suddenly woke to a loud thud. He had kicked over the pot of flour.

Moral: Dreams can never become reality.

THE CAP SELLER AND THE MONKEYS

There was once a cap seller who sold caps in different towns and villages. He travelled a long way each day on foot, carrying a huge basket full of caps. One hot day he was crossing the woods. He was very tired.

The poor cap seller was so tired that the moment he put his heavy basket aside and lay down, he fell fast asleep.

As the poor cap seller lay fast asleep, a group of monkeys that lived in the forest came down from the trees. They were attracted by the colourful caps, and started playing with them.

Suddenly, the cap seller woke up with a start. He was shocked to see the monkeys playing with his caps. Seeing him awake the monkeys scampered up the trees with the caps.

The cap seller was very angry when he saw that the monkeys had snatched away his caps. He pointed his finger at them and shouted angrily. The monkeys immediately imitated him.

The cap seller was a very clever man. He realised that the monkeys would imitate whatever he did. He had an idea. He took a cap and wore it on his head. The monkeys immediately did the same with the caps they had snatched.

The clever cap seller then took the cap off his head and threw it on the ground. Seeing him, the monkeys did the same with the caps on their heads.

The clever cap seller gathered all the caps the monkeys had thrown down and put them back into his basket. Then he put the basket on his head and went on his way to the next village.

Moral: Wisdom always prevails over foolishness.

THE CROW AND THE JACKAL

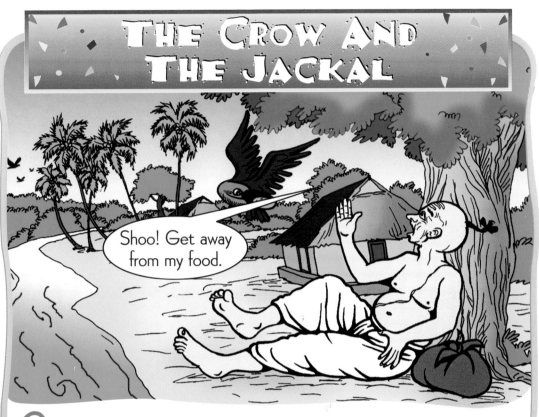

Shoo! Get away from my food.

Once a crow saw an old Brahmin eating some bread. The crow was very hungry. When the Brahmin was looking away, she quickly snatched a piece of bread and flew away with it.

The hungry crow flew away to a tree in the woods nearby and sat down to eat the tasty piece of bread.

Just then, a jackal came up from behind. He saw the crow sitting on the tree with the bread in her beak. The jackal was a very cunning and greedy animal. He wanted to have the bread.

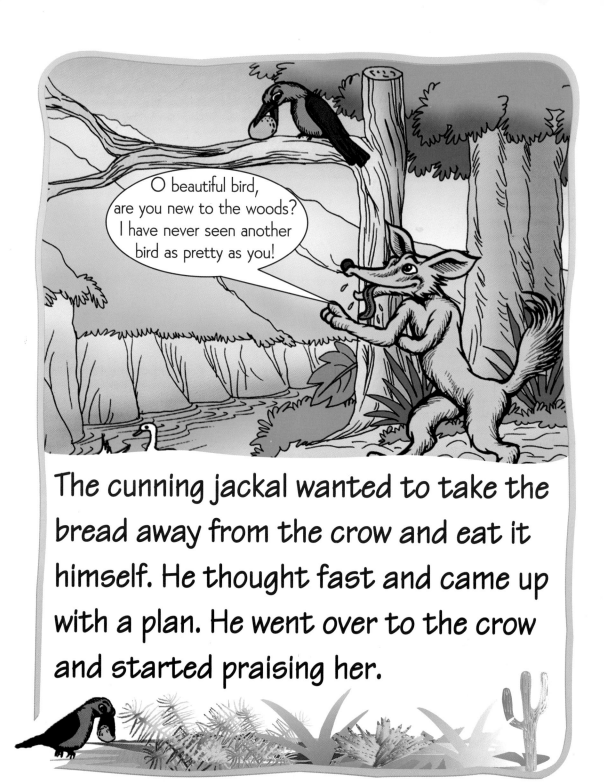

The cunning jackal wanted to take the bread away from the crow and eat it himself. He thought fast and came up with a plan. He went over to the crow and started praising her.

At first the crow ignored the jackal. She knew that the jackal was a cunning animal. But the jackal did not give up. He praised her even more.

After a while, the crow began to feel flattered. She had never heard so many nice things being said about her. She even started believing the jackal's words.

The crow listened to the jackal's words of flattery and started to believe that she could sing. She decide to sing. Just as she opened her beak to sing, the bread fell from her beak, only to be snapped up by the cunning jackal.

It was only then that the poor crow realised that she had been tricked by the cunning jackal. As she looked helplessly, the jackal mocked her and went away with the piece of bread.

Moral: Flattery is the weapon of the cunning.

THE BARBER AND THE SAINTS

I had a strange dream last night.

Once a pious and generous man fell into bad times. He lost all his wealth. One night he had a strange dream. He dreamed that a saint who came to his house turned into a heap of gold when touched on the head with a stick.

The pious man believed in dreams. So the next morning he waited anxiously to see if the dream would come true. Suddenly he heard the sound of footsteps.

At first the pious man was disappointed. It was only the barber. But as he sat down for his shave, a saint came to his house. The pious man could not believe his eyes.

It really was the dream coming true. The saint bowed before him. When the pious man touched his head with a stick the saint turned into a heap of gold. The barber who saw all this was filled with surprise.

The ignorant barber had a plan. He invited some saints from a hermitage for a feast. Hoping they would turn into gold, he began hitting the poor saints over the head with a stout stick.

One of the saints managed to escape from the greedy barber and informed the king's guards. They rushed to the barber's house and took him away to the king who punished him for his greed.

Moral: Think before you act.

THE CRANE AND THE CRAB

One day in the forest, a crane stood at the edge of a pond looking sad and thoughtful. But in his mind he had a wicked plan.

The fishes of the pond were sorry when they saw the crane looking so sad. They asked him what was the reason for his sadness. The crane told them that he was a soothsayer and that he could see into the future.

All the fishes were filled with fear.
But there was one crab in the pond
who did not believe the crane's story.

But the foolish fishes did not listen to the crab. They asked the crane to help them escape from the pond.

So the crane carried one fish to the lake and brought him back. When the fish told the others about how big and deep the other lake was, they were all anxious to go there.

But the crane did not take them to the lake. One after another, the crane took the fishes to a tree near by. He ate them up and threw the bones down.

When there were no fishes left, the crane offered to carry the crab to the lake. Since he was too big for the crane's beak, the crab held on to the crane's long neck with his strong claws.

Suddenly the crab saw that the crane was flying towards a tree. At the bottom of the tree was a heap of fish bones. The crab realised that the crane had killed all the poor fishes. Using his strong claws, the crab choked the wicked crane to death.

Moral: Evil to him that evil plots.

Best Selling Titles From Shree

Fun With Phonics

Learn and Enjoy Series

Fun with colour

 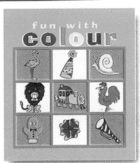

Panchatantra Series

Best Selling Titles from Shree

Character Builder Series

 Thomo And Kyle

 Huber And The Thief

 Careh And Her Friends

 Nosey And The Fox

 Goran And His Adventure

 Ted And The Bicycle

 Sarah, Carl And The Party

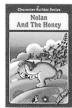 Nolan And The Honey

Shakespeare

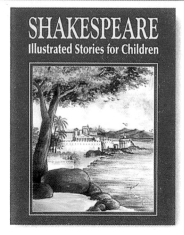

SHAKESPEARE
Illustrated Stories for Children

Animal Moral Stories

 Ralph And The Time

 Tru And Fib

 Monty And The Thieves

 Nyce And Nasti

 The Jackal And The Tiger

 Percy And His Pranks

 Frisky And Slobby

 Jim And His Friends

Stories from Panchatantra

LARGE PRINT
Stories From
PANCHATANTRA

Animal Adventure Stories

 Mike And The Bunny

 Sue, Hayden And The Raft

 Jack And The Treasure

 Kathy And The Time Machine

 Zender And The Glowing Toy

 Fret And Polly

 Wooly And The Magic Glasses

 Robbie And Dean

More Stories from Panchatantra

LARGE PRINT
More Stories From
PANCHATANTRA